A FLIGHT OF MARCEAU

MoonsMoon

BY
JOE BROWN

ILLUSTRATIONS BY STEPHEN MARCHESI

MAJESTIC EAGLE PUBLISHING CO.
CHICAGO, ILLINOIS

To my thirteen grandchildren,
Sydney, Sloan, Ross, Duke, Gabe, Maxx, C.J., Sam, Zach, Jake, Jessie, Cody and Dylan,
most of whom helped me write this book;
my daughter, Bobbi, who restarted my motor; my daughter, Linda, who helps keep it running;
and to my best friend, Lola, who also happens to be my wife.
(How lucky am I?)

Published by
Majestic Eagle Publishing Co.
6649 Navajo
Lincolnwood, IL 60712

TheFlightsofMarceau.com

Second Printing 2013
Printed in USA

Library of Congress Cataloging in Publication Data
Joe Brown, 1935–
Moonsmoon–A Flight of Marceau

ISBN 978-0-9797495-5-1

DESIGNED BY MARY KORNBLUM, CMYK DESIGN INC.
PRODUCED BY DELLA R. MANCUSO, MANCUSO ASSOCIATES INC.

Marceau is my name and I'm driving a cab

And my mind does me proud to escape from the drab

For the world as I know it is tired and dry

 But my mind lets me leap to the heights of the sky...

 Drab = dreary

Heights = top

Good morning, old pal
Please get into the car
The rear door is open, I have left it ajar
I have a story this morning, that you ought to hear
It's one of the strangest of my entire career.

Though it may bring me some well-deserved glory
I am somewhat reluctant to tell you this story
I've had trouble deciding if I should tell you or not …
But you're a really great kid, so I'll give it a shot

Ajar = slightly open

Deserved = earned
Reluctant = careful

Now, please listen closely and heed my words well   Heed = pay attention

I can tell you a story that you never can tell

It's a tale I've kept hidden way high on a shelf

You must promise to keep this one all to yourself

Let's look all around us before we begin

To make certain that nobody's listening in.   Certain = real sure

It's a story about animals that none of us see
Though they once lived on earth and were happy and free
But alas, they're now gone and I miss them all greatly

Alas = too bad

Have any of you seen a Unicorn lately?
I know you've seen pictures in all of your books
But let me tell you, firsthand, how a Unicorn looks

Firsthand = I saw it

They're like beautiful horses, sleek and well fed

Sleek = shiny, smooth

They have big blue eyes and a horn on their head

For all of their lives they stay active and spry

Spry = active

With smiles on their faces and a gleam in their eye

And what's important to a Unicorn? What's number one?

Goal = aim, desire

They believe the main goal of life is to have lots of fun.

ℬut they've been in need of a home where Unicorns play
Ever since Noah forgot them that long ago day
On that day they were busy at play in the park
And lost track of the time and were late for the ark.   Ark = Noah's boat

So they were left all alone, the future was bleak   Bleak = dreary
The flood would engulf them in less than a week   Engulf = drown
But those Unicorns, who were so greatly adored   Adored = loved
Were saved from the flood and received their reward.

Their own beautiful planet, that was as safe as could be
Well hidden from earth, to keep it happy and free
You can't see it from here, it's there behind the moon
It was hidden so that no one would come visiting soon
This place was called Moonsmoon, if you get what I mean
It's a moon of our moon that will never be seen.

There is everything there that a unicorn needs

Like big, bright, red cherries and succulent reeds   Succulent = juicy

Sweet tangerines and apples galore   Reeds = plants

They have all that they need, never hunger for more   Galore = a lot

They can eat what they want, whenever they want

Their beloved Moonsmoon was their own restaurant

Wherever you looked, fresh, pure water flowed

That is destined forever to run clear and cold.   Destined = certain

Well, I've been to that place that the Unicorns share
But no one else knows that there's anything there
So, it's time for the story you've been waiting to hear
There'll be no bad guys involved nor anywhere near
Still, the problem was one of the worst that I've had
Although nobody meant to do anything bad.

A moon shot had been scheduled early one day
And a crew of brave astronauts were sent on their way
Their target, the moon, they had been there before
But they could never imagine what might be in store
They thought they could get there in one afternoon
But made a tiny mistake and flew right past the moon.

It was the strangest of things, but when they flew into space
They saw this unknown, incredible, beautiful place
They had come across Moonsmoon quite by mistake
Who knew what direction their adventure might take?
So they decided to stop, for whatever it's worth
Until it was time to return to their base on the earth.

When they landed they came out and looked all around
They saw Unicorns playing and pawing the ground
Running and jumping and laughing with glee
As happy as Unicorns ever could be.

Glee = happiness

But once man arrived it didn't take long
For things to start going incredibly wrong
One of the crew didn't cover his face
When he was sneezing and coughing all over the place
Well, a really big problem was caused by that man
There had never been sickness since Moonsmoon began.

But when the man walked around and sneezed in the air
The flu bug decided that it liked it out there.

Over Moonsmoon it traveled, biting the young and the old
Soon every single Unicorn came down with a cold
The flu bugs then spread with the greatest of ease
Until the Unicorns of Moonsmoon all fell to their knees.

Flu bug = germs

They went to their beds, coughin' and sneezin'
And they shivered all over as if they were freezin'
All the Unicorns cried, they could not lift their heads
They were even too weak to get out of their beds.

If something wasn't done, it would be a shock to behold
Because Unicorns can easily die from a cold
It wouldn't take long, a few days at the most
And we didn't want a Unicorn to turn into a ghost.

So, Ulysses the Unicorn, the boss of them all
Dragged out of his bed to make one frantic call   Frantic = excited
He chose to call Pegasus, you can easily see why
Since the winged horse lives closest to them in the sky
You remember Pegasus, the horse with the wings
He could always be counted on for the important things.

Pegasus said, "I think I can help, so I'd better go
The smartest thing to do is go pick up Marceau."
Well, that's just what he did, and after saying "Hello"
He explained the whole problem and where I must go.

Then Marceau gathered medicine galore
And hoped that he needn't come back for more.
Pegasus said, "We will soon be there."
And with a burst of energy soared into the air
We flew to Moonsmoon, nothing got in our way
It's amazing how quickly we got there that day.

Galore = a lot

Soared = flew high, easily

I hadn't the slightest idea of what was in store
But when I saw it my jaw almost dropped to the floor
In the sky there were rainbows wherever you look
Like pictures you've seen in a library book
I saw fruit-covered branches against a crystal blue sky
And a fluffy white cloud with a tear in its eye.

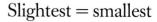
Slightest = smallest

I stood there astounded, my mouth open wide

Astounded = amazed

While a feeling of wonder soon filled me inside

But I had the serum upon which their life depends

Serum = medicine

So I rushed to the beds of my Unicorn friends

Each received a flu shot and a little penicillin

Flu shot, penicillin = medicine

Marceau then departed to search for the villain.

Villain = bad guy

Listening more closely, I heard somebody wheezing
And followed the sound of the coughing and sneezing
The noises were strange so I snuck up behind
But there were no villains for Marceau to find.

I came upon an astronaut, her name-tag said "Marie"
She was sitting very calmly, just sipping at her tea
She was so surprised to see me, her tea spilled on the ground
Marie was not aware that anyone was anywhere around.

Aware = knew

"Do you know what you did here was strictly taboo?"   Taboo = no-no

"No, I really don't know," she said. "What did I do?"

"Did you notice that the Unicorns have become very ill?

Well, they all would have died if it weren't for the pill.

The sickness was spread by the coughing and sneezing

And the germs in the air that were not very pleasing."

"What a terrible thing," she said, very contrite.   Contrite = sorry

"What can we do to make everything right?"

"The best you can do is to leave right away

And please do not sneeze 'til you're well on your way."

Then the Unicorns begged us to never reveal
The secret of Moonsmoon they wished to conceal
Because if people found out that it really existed
The flu might return and they couldn't resist it.

Reveal = tell
Conceal = hide
Existed = was real
Resist = fight back

When they realized what had happened, why the Unicorns fell
The astronauts swore that they never would tell
For they knew if they told it would be so very wrong
It would bring sickness and Moonsmoon wouldn't last very long
For the Unicorns there, that would be the end of the game
They would die and be gone, what a terrible shame.

Now you've got the whole story, please watch what you say
So that Unicorns will always be out of harm's way
Just remember your promise, don't let anyone know
If we keep it a secret then no one will go …

We have come to the end of this incredible show
And I'm glad that you enjoyed this true tale of Marceau
The unicorns, my friend, are depending on you
So don't breathe a word of this, whatever you do.

About the author

JOE BROWN lives in the village of Lincolnwood, Illinois, with his wife, Lola. He was an attorney in Chicago for fifty years before embarking on a writing career at age 70. Bop, as he is known in the family, started writing these stories for his children in the 1960s. After retiring he began, again, writing about Marceau's adventures. Moonsmoon is his seventh children's book.

About the artist

STEPHEN MARCHESI has illustrated numerous picture books, text-books and magazines. A graduate of Pratt Institute, his books have been on the Children's Book Council bestsellers list and on the Bank Street College Children's Book of the Year lists. He lives with his wife and son in Croton-on-Hudson, New York.

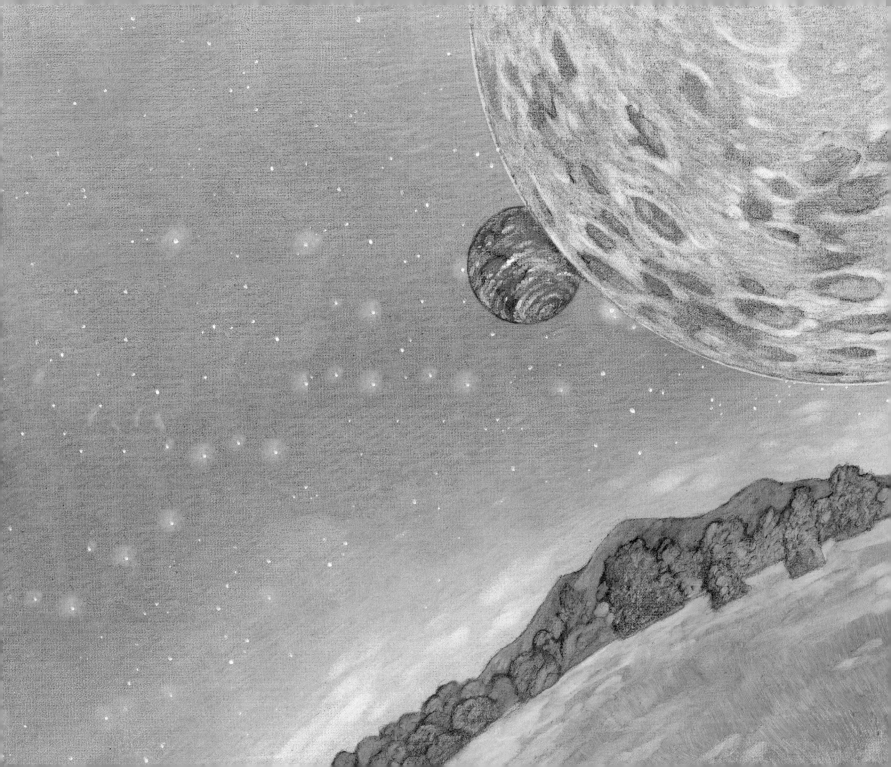